THE ANIMAL STORYBOOK

SUZIE SIDDONS

Illustrated by
ROWAN CLIFFORD

TREASURE PRESS

KT-364-756

Once upon a time there was a zoo.

It was a very popular zoo and every day hundreds of people queued up to pay their money and pass through the turnstiles to see the animals.

There were many different animals to see; lions and tigers, penguins and elephants, raccoons, frilled lizards, pelicans, hyenas and wallabies – in fact, the same animals that are in zoos all over the world. There was a reptile house and a large aquarium and a wonderful bird house.

The animals were well looked after by their keepers. The head keeper was called Mr Wellbeloved and he was just like his name suggests he was. The animals liked him enormously. He had lots of assistant keepers and assistant assistant keepers.

The animals were fed two times a day. People flocked to where the penguins lived, and laughed and applauded as the funny black and white birds expertly caught all the fish thrown at them.

The chimpanzees were popular, too, at feeding time. They sat round a table and had cups and saucers, just like real people – only their table manners were disgraceful. In fact they behaved like lots of children would like to but are not allowed to.

There were large notices all around saying 'Please do not feed the animals', but occasionally the animals helped themselves to a bun.

The animals' cages were cleaned regularly.

The animals enjoyed watching the humans watching them. One day the hyenas were laughing at a lady laughing at them. She laughed so hard that she swallowed her false teeth. This made the hyenas laugh even harder.

The animals all loved having their photographs taken. Whenever any of them saw a camera being produced, they would stop whatever they were doing and smile and pose for the people taking the photographs. The chimpanzees were especially good at this and there were always crowds of people around their cages, snapping happily.

Occasionally, some of the humans were unkind to the animals. There was a little boy once who kept on making faces at all of them. He was standing in front of the elephants one day watching them taking a drink. Suddenly one of them sneezed and the boy was drenched. The hyenas laughed and laughed until they thought they were going to fall over, and the chimpanzees wished that they'd had a camera to take a snapshot of it.

At night, when the zoo was closed and the keeper, the assistant keepers and their assistants had gone home to enjoy their free time, the animals would slip out of their pens and cages and enclosures and gather together to tell stories.

And sometimes, when the zoo was closed for the day they would get up to all sorts of things . . .

A bout turn, left wheel. Keep in step there!' The adjutant stork's voice carried clearly across the grass where the stork army were practising marching one day after the zoo had closed.

All the animals gathered to watch and the little tiger cub joined in behind the line of storks, stamping along, trying to imitate the birds.

After about five minutes he became bored.

'Why do they all march together?' he asked his mother.

'Wait until later,' said the tigress, 'you'll find out then.'

An hour or two later the animals gathered round the adjutant stork, and all the other storks stood to attention as he cleared his throat ready to begin.

'Years ago, me and my men, my brave men, were happily fishing in our usual place. We'd fished there for years without any trouble. There was plenty of fish and no one bothered us. Suddenly we were invaded by the flamingoes. Came at us like wolves. Wave after wave of 'em, determined to drive us away.

'We defended as best we could, but there were too many of 'em, too many. So we fled to the hills. Beaten! There we all got together, what we military birds call regrouping, to discuss what to do or, in military terms, tactics.

'One of my brave lads volunteered to go back as a spy. Volunteered he did! He only had to be told to do it twice too! He disguised himself with leaves and twigs and crept down to the water's edge in the dark. When the sun came

up, there he was, standing still and straight, just like
a eucalyptus bush. Thank goodness there were none of
you dogs about at the time. All day he stood there
listening to the flamingoes boasting about their victory.
He couldn't help but notice that they spent most of their time
preening themselves. If as much as a speck of dirt landed on them,
they had a fit. Vain birds flamingoes. Very vain.

'When night came he crept back to our camp to report.
Suddenly I hit on it . . . our plan that is. All that night we practised,
marched and marched, drilled and drilled. Our flying forces
practised flight tactics until we were perfect. Perfect we were.

'We set off at dawn. All of us armed . . . or should I say winged
. . . sorry, just my little joke . . . with mud. Thick black sticky mud. The
first wave of bombers flew in, in perfect formation. They flew in low
and fast and let the flamingoes have it. Fifty of 'em went down in the
first strike. Covered in mud they were. Covered. Then we sent in our
foot soldiers. Worked like clockwork it did. Clockwork. The
flamingoes who had already been hit were too busy trying to get the
mud off themselves to care about their mates. Our army marched
through the mud, throwing it up in great lumps and every lump
found its mark on a flamingo.

'They signed a peace treaty with us and never poached our
waters again. Mind you, we still keep the patrols up just in case.
You never know when they might try it again.'

All the animals clapped enthusiastically. All, that is apart
from the flamingoes. They had been too busy preening
themselves to pay attention.

'Tonight,' came the message from the lion one day, 'we will meet at the Reptile House and the rattlesnake shall tell us a tale.' So when evening came, the animals made their way across the grass by the monkey's cages, through the tunnel under the sea lion's pool and into the cool, quiet house where the snakes lived.

The little tiger cub had never known his mother to be afraid of anything before, so he was surprised to see how frightened she looked. All the animals seemed subdued and indeed many of them had not come at all.

The polar bear said that he had a dreadful cold and would stay behind. The giraffe's throat was so sore that he said that he would go to bed early.

The animals gathered round the glass case where the king rattlesnake lived. The tiger cub noticed that they did not go too close, and not one of them went up to the glass and pressed their nose against it.

The rattlesnake had a whispery and scratchy voice and the animals sat very still as he told his tale.

'I am the king of all the snakes,' he began. 'I know that the cobra claims to be king, but the mongoose can defeat him. There is no animal that can defeat me. I am King.'

'But there is one animal who can get the better of you, isn't there?' growled the lion sternly. 'An animal who can control all of us if he puts his mind to it. Never forget that.'

'Who is that Mum?' asked the tiger cub.

'Hush dear,' said his mother, 'listen to the snake's story.'

'After the rain came down and while all our ancestors were in the Ark,' the rattlesnake went on, 'My ever-so-many-greats-great-grandfather was bored. No one wanted to sleep next to him; I can't think why, but there it was. Now when he

was bored he got bad tempered. He couldn't resist biting Mrs Noah when she came along with her broom. And what a fuss she made! Even though it was only a little nibble. You would have thought the roof had come off the Ark! Noah was furious! Naturally my ever-so-many-greats-great-grandfather slithered away and hid to wait until the uproar died down. This only made Mrs Noah angrier.

"If that snake's not found, I won't be able to sleep a wink!" she screamed, and then started on about one of her headaches coming on. Apparently Noah got very peculiar when his wife had one of her headaches, so that started the Great Hunt. All the other snakes were captured and kept in sacks for the rest of the voyage. But my ever-so-many-greats-great-grandfather had hidden himself so well that no one found him.

'Now when the dove came back with the olive branch from Mount Ararat, my ever-so-many-greats-great-grandfather knew that pretty soon all the animals would be leaving. He was sure that in all the hustle and bustle he would be able to slip away unnoticed. He'd nearly made it when Noah spotted him. Quick as a flash, Noah threw his cloak over him and that was when my ever-so-many-greats-great-grandfather learned that man was the only animal who could get the better of him. And a hard lesson it was to learn too.'

'But what did Noah do to him?' asked the tiger cub nervously. 'This,' said the rattlesnake, holding up his tail. 'He put a rattle in his tail so that he could never hide again.'

11

'M um,' asked the little tiger curiously, 'why are all tigers stripey?'

'Well now,' his mother answered, 'it's strange that you should ask me that, because tonight I'm going to tell everyone why.'And later that evening she settled down to tell her tale.

'Now my dears,' she began, looking all around her and blinking lazily. 'I shall tell you exactly why tigers have stripes. You see, the very first tigers were covered with soft fur which was all spotted – just like my handsome son here used to be – but as the tigers grew they started to argue about what sort of coat they wanted when they were fully grown. You know how children are ... The boy cub wanted to have a golden coat like the lion but the girl cub wanted a dark glossy coat like the black panther.

'"A beautiful black coat will show off my lovely yellow eyes," she said. "Yes, that is what I shall have when I am fully grown." She was a vain little thing.

'"But I want a golden coat," said the boy cub. "I want to stalk amongst the yellow grass and a black coat would be far too noticeable for that."

'And so they argued and argued and neither would give way. When at last they were fully grown they each had a coat of the colour that they had chosen, and very useful they were too. The tiger hunted in the daytime when his yellow coat was hidden by the dry yellow grass of the plains, and the tigress hunted at night, where only the gleam of her yellow eyes showed where she was. And so things went on and they lived together fairly peaceably. But when the time came for the first tigers to have their first litter of cubs the arguments started again.

'The male tiger was determined that the cubs should be like him and the female was determined that they should be like her.

'"Wouldn't it be nice if they had yellow coats," said the father?

'"Much better that

they had black coats,'' said the mother.

'"Our cubs *shall* have yellow coats like me,'' said the father tiger, "and then they can hunt in the daytime.''

'"Oh no they *won't*,'' said the mother tiger, ''they will have black coats like me and will hunt at night.''

'So the quarrelling went on and on until the day that the cubs were born. Their parents looked at them in horror, for all their cubs had spotty coats, just as they had once had.' The tigress paused . . .

'Go on Mum,' said the little tiger cub. 'What happened then, what sort of coats did they have in the end?'

'I'm coming to that,' said the tigress. 'The cubs grew up with coats that were equally striped in black and gold, and all tigers since then have been the same.'

'But what about the hunting in the daytime and at night?' asked the little tiger cub. 'What happened to that?'

'They came to an understanding,' said the tigress, 'and since then, tigers have only hunted during the hours of morning and evening when the golden light of the sun and the black shadows of the night are equally shared – just like their coats.'

'But tigers don't hunt in zoos,' said the tiger cubs.

'I know,' said the tigress 'such a pity. I always wanted a black fur coat.'

The next evening was fine and clear but very windy. As the animals again gathered to hear the story, the wind blew aside the leaves of the large tree that stood by the lion's den. Up among the leaves there was an animal, hanging from a branch like a brown bag of washing and swaying slightly.

'Who's that Mum?' asked the smallest tiger cub, 'I've never seen *him* before.'

'That's the sloth dear,' she answered.

'Is he going to tell the story tonight?' asked the cub.

'If he is we'll be here a long time,' she replied, 'so you'd better snuggle up close in case you get sleepy.'

Slowly, slowly the sloth came down out of the tree, and slowly, slowly he came down to the group of animals. Slowly, slowly he lay down and put his feet into the air.

'I'm more comfortable like this ...' he said in his slow, slurred voice. 'This way I can look ... out ... for ... rain. If it wasn't for us sloths Noah would never have found the other animals ... sloths were the first animals into the ark you know ...'

'Tell us about it,' begged the tiger cub. 'I haven't heard this story before.' The animals sat back to listen and the sloth began.

'Sloths didn't always live in the trees ... once we romped about on the land ... just like the rest of you.'

'Romped about indeed!' jeered the cheetah. 'Watching you romping must have been like watching a rock romping about.' And he frisked around just to show how light on his feet he was.

'Well ... it ... was ... romping to my ancestors ...' the sloth went on, 'some of them romped fast and some of them romped slowly, and that's just ... the way ... it was. As I was saying, they didn't live in the trees, although they always wanted to climb them. But the trouble was, they didn't know how to climb ... My ancestors had been abandoned by their parents, so you see there was no one to teach them how to climb. Even when they were grown up, they still didn't know how to climb trees.

So ... when the first plague of locusts came, the sloths were in a very bad way. Nasty little things ... locusts. Crawl along the ground they do, and eat

14

everything they meet. Well there was nothing for it, my ancestors had to learn tree climbing – there and then. They did very well, considering it was the first time, but when they got there, they were hanging upside down and simply could not work out how to get themselves the right way up. The locusts passed by and it was then that it began to rain. My ancestors kept on saying how much it was raining, but no one paid them any attention ... just went on romping about and romping about. But after about three days it had rained so much that they started to take notice and romped away to the higher ground, leaving my ancestors hanging there as the waters rose and rose.

'That was where Noah found them ... and he took them into the Ark. He made them a lovely tree house so they could live on the roof because they'd got used to hanging upside down by then you see.

'Since that day sloths have never romped about, just kept ourselves to ourselves, hanging up in the trees ... looking out for rain ...'

'I don't believe a word of it', said the cheetah.

'It's true ... I ... assure ... you,' said the sloth.

'Humph!' snorted the cheetah.

'Anyway,' said the sloth, 'that's my story and I'm sticking to it.'

'There now dear,' said the tigress, 'wasn't that a nice story?'

But there was no answer from her son – the smallest tiger had fallen asleep.

But I want to be number six,' said the little tiger cub grumpily, trying to chew at the big number three on his back. 'Why can't I be number six?'

'Because the sports committee have better things to do than change all the numbers just to suit one little tiger cub,' answered his mother patiently. 'Now go and get into line for the obstacle race.'

It was the keeper's day off and the zoo was closed. So the animals had decided to hold their Sports Day.

The tiger cub romped across to the starting line and stood between the smallest hippo and the youngest armadillo. The other animals in the race were the little elephant, the gnu twins and the Galapagos turtle triplets.

The sloth lay very still with his legs in the air, holding the starting pistol in his front paws.

Spats McLean the alligator, who was acting as the referee, stepped forward carrying a megaphone.

'On your marks ...' he called, 'Ready ... Steady ... GO! ......
But not a sound came from the starting pistol.

'Come along, come along,' Spats shouted through the megaphone at the sloth, who seemed to be asleep.

'Don't ... hurry ... me,' said the sloth slowly, 'all ... in ... good ... time.'

One of the gnu twins, who had been eagerly leaning forward, overbalanced and fell over the starting line.

'Ready ...' began Spats again, '... Steady ... GO!'

This time the starting pistol did go off – much to the amazement of the sloth who gazed up at it as if it had bitten him.

The young animals scampered off towards the first obstacle, a hollow log. The tiger cub scrambled through first, closely followed by the gnu twins with the armadillo and the hippo behind them. Then came the young elephant.

'Come on Geoffrey,' trumpeted his mother and father, as the little elephant huffed and puffed his way into the log.

Now the little elephant was only 'little' compared to other elephants – compared to the rest of the young competitors he wasn't little at all. Half way through, Geoffrey got stuck with his head, trunk, ears and front legs sticking out of one end of the log and his back legs and tail out of the other. Not that this bothered Geoffrey, he lumbered on, leaving the Galapagos triplets gaping at him.

'Disqualified! 7, 8 and 9!' boomed Spats, through the megaphone. 'For not going through the first obstacle.'

'But that's not fair ...' began the triplets, 'Geoffrey's run off in the first obstacle.'

'The referee's decision is final,' snapped Spats as three of his henchmen carried the triplets away from the course.

The watching animals began to murmur amongst themselves.

The tiger cub ran on, closely followed by the hippo, the gnu twins, the armadillo and of course Geoffrey, whose number was now hidden by the hollow log.

The next obstacle was a net slung between two trees. The tiger cub scrambled over it, closely followed by the hippo and the gnus. The twins were half way over and the armadillo was just about to climb onto the net when Geoffrey lumbered past him and into it, tearing it away from the trees as it wrapped itself wildly around his ears, with the gnu twins still tangled up in it.

'Disqualified, numbers 5 and 6 for riding on the back of another competitor,' roared Spats through the megaphone, 'AND number 4, for not climbing the second obstacle.'

'But that's not fair!' said the gnu twins in muffled voices from the net.

'No it's not!' said the smallest armadillo. 'Geoffrey has carried away the second obstacle.'

'And us with it,' wailed the twins mournfully.

'The referee's decision is final!' said Spats angrily as some of the watching animals began to hiss and boo at him.

Still the tiger cub and the hippo raced on until they came to the third obstacle – a small lake. The tiger cub dived in and swam to the other side. Geoffrey and the little hippo arrived at the lake at the same moment and before the hippo could jump in, Geoffrey lowered his trunk into the water and drank the lake dry.

'Disqualified, number 2!' boomed Spats through the megaphone, 'for not swimming the third obstacle.'

'But that's not fair,' squeaked the little hippo. 'Geoffrey's drunk the third obstacle.'

'The referee's decision is final,' snapped Spats as his three henchmen carried the little hippo away. The hissing and booing grew louder and the animals gathered round Spats.

And still the race went on. The tiger cub darted forward to the last obstacle – a high brick wall. He sprang onto it and jumped down to the other side just as Geoffrey ran straight through the wall,

scattering bricks right and left, with the net round his ears, the hollow log round his middle and the water from the lake sloshing and splashing inside him.

'Disqualified, number 3!' boomed Spats.

'What for?' said the tiger cub indignantly as he crossed the finishing line just ahead of Geoffrey.

'For ... for ... winning ... er ... no, for, er, letting Geoffrey knock the wall down. The referee's decision is ...'

'Were you about to say "final", Spats dear?' said the tigress quietly, unsheathing her claws and examining them carefully.

'Are you sure you mean "final", Spats dear?' said the mother armadillo, rattling her platelets elegantly.

'Are you *really certain* you mean "final", Spats dear?' said the mother gnu, lowering her head gracefully so that the sun glinted on her sharp horns.

'Well,' said Spats nervously, 'if you put it like that, I suppose I shall have to give the cup to the tiger.'

At this there came a great wail from Geoffrey.

'But you told me that *I* was going to win, Uncle Spats,' sobbed the little elephant. 'What about all those buns that my Dad gave you to make sure that you didn't forget? I never win anything. I'm fat and ugly and I never do anything right ...' and Geoffrey broke down in a flood of tears.

The tiger cub went over to Geoffrey and snuggled up against him,

'Don't cry,' the little cub said kindly. 'Here, you can share the cup with me and I'll explain all about obstacle races to you so that you'll know what to do next time. Now the thing about obstacles is that although they're in your way, you have to get over them properly, it's a bit like ...'

'Like mumps or measles?' asked Geoffrey.

'Well not eggzackly ...' went on the tiger cub ...

19

One night, all the animals had been waiting for ages to hear a story when the tiger cub saw a large pair of ears appearing and disappearing suddenly among the leaves. It turned out to be the wallaby.

He was covered with twigs and leaves and pieces of sticking plaster. His right forepaw was clumsily bandaged and his left arm was in a sling. He couldn't keep still for a moment. He bounced from side to side. Bumping into the elephant and sometimes knocking the flamingoes about as if they were a pile of umbrellas. The sloth looked on approvingly.

'Now that's what I call romping,' he muttered to himself.

'Well,' began the wallaby breathlessly, 'I suppose you want to know why we wallabies have a pouch on our fronts. It happened like this ... Wallabies have always been accident prone. That's why Noah dropped the pair in the Ark off in Australia. It's a very large place and rather bare so there aren't too many things to bump into. At first it was a bit difficult being upside down, but we soon got used to it and now we think we're the right way up.

'"Here," the first mother wallaby said to her son one day, "you'd better carry a bandage with you, since you're always needing one," and she handed him a roll of bandage. He took it firmly in his right paw and set off.

'Well, he hadn't gone far when the bandage started to unroll, and the more it unrolled the more it tangled about his feet until at last he tumbled over it and banged his head on a rock and fell into a thorn bush.

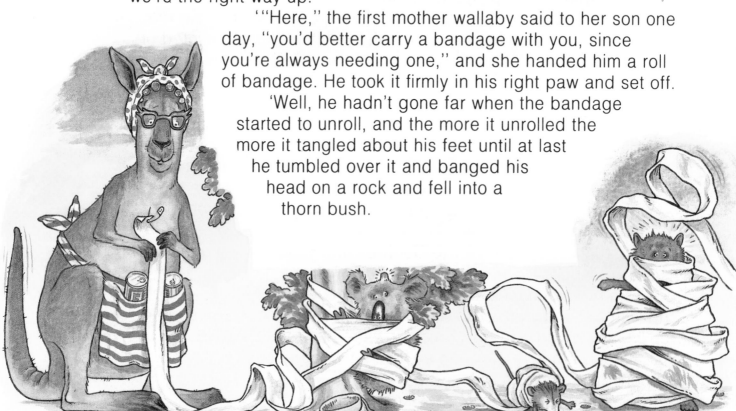

'When he didn't come home that night all his mother had to do was follow the trail of bandage until she found him.

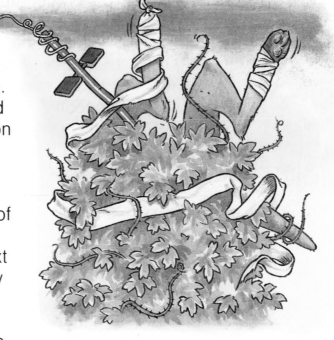

'After she had bandaged his bruises and put plaster on his cuts she said to him, "You'd better carry both of these," and she handed him another bandage and a roll of sticking plaster.

'Off he set again the next day, but he hadn't gone very far when the other bandage started to unroll and the sticking plaster melted in the heat and stuck his hands together, and of course over he tumbled and bumped his head again, and grazed his knee and scraped his ear.

'Well you can imagine how cross his mother was, so she made him a nice little pouch to keep his supplies in.

'Since then all we wallabies have had nice little pouches for really essential things.'

'What kind of things?' asked the little tiger cub.

'Oh, real essentials like bandages and sticking plasters!' answered the wallaby, and bounced away.

A long time ago, before Noah built his Ark,' said the raccoon one night, 'my ancestors had a wonderful idea.'

'That was probably the last idea a raccoon had,' muttered the lion.

'Do you want to hear this story, or not,' asked the raccoon.

'I suppose so' replied the lion.

'Well be quiet and listen.'

The animals settled down to listen to the raccoon.

'It was like this,' started the raccoon. 'The raccoons saw that lots of the animals were unhappy with the way they looked.'

'Hardly surprising really,' said a peacock preening itself proudly.

The raccoon ignored this remark and carried on.

'At first everything worked well. Any animal that wanted to change its appearance went to the little shop that was opened and was put in touch with another animal who wanted to change. They were charged a small fee, of course, and everyone was quite happy.

'Then along comes the alligators,' the raccoon went on looking across at Spats Maclean, who immediately looked away.

'The alligators persuaded the raccoons that the business needed expanding and offered to work for them in a large warehouse. The raccoons were quite happy with this. They would be getting more money for less work. So they opened this huge warehouse and built up a store of skins. The animals could come in and try them on at their leisure and take their time deciding what they wanted.

'The alligators put up large notices advertising the warehouse and soon they were as busy as anything.

'Then one day along comes a new manager. Harry his name was. And if you think Spats is crooked you should have met his ancestor. It was then that things began to go wrong.

'First of all two tortoises came in. Furious they were. Not surprising really. You see tortoises used to have the most beautiful golden coats. Really thick they were. But this pair were wearing old coal scuttles. Claimed they had had their skins taken from them at the warehouse and had had to wear the scuttles to cover themselves.

'Harry calmed them down. Said their coats had been temporarily mislaid and pointed out that the scuttles would be useful if it rained before the coats turned up.

'Then along comes two armadillos. Next to the tortoises, armadillos had the second most beautiful coats, but this pair were wearing old suits of armour. They told Harry that when they'd turned round the coats had been stolen.

'Now just then the rains started and old Noah comes along to get all the animals into the Ark. The only two tortoises he could find were the two in the old coal scuttles and the only two armadillos he could find were the two in the armour. And that's why tortoises today have shells and armadillos have armour plating.'

'Wasn't Noah angry when he found out what had happened?' asked the tiger cub.

'Angry? He was furious. It seemed that Harry had been stealing coats left, right and centre and that lots of the animals that used to have really thick coats had had them stolen and been forced to wear any old thing they could find. But old Noah got his own back on the alligators. You see three alligators managed to get on to the Ark. Harry, his wife and his father-in-law. The old alligator didn't make it to dry land. He died half way through the voyage. So old Noah used *his* skin and made Mrs Noah a lovely handbag and matching shoes. Ever since then women have always liked alligator skin shoes and bags.'

Just then the raccoon noticed that Spats was trying to hide something behind his back. 'What's that Spats,' he shouted.

'Oh it's nothing,' said Spats. 'Just an old coat that fell off the back of a loris.'

It had been raining all day – absolutely pouring down, and no one had come to the zoo. The patch of grass in front of the lions' den was drenched.

'Do you think that Noah will have to build another Ark?' asked the tiger cub, huddling up against his mother.

'I shouldn't think so,' his mother answered, and a drop of rain trickled down her right ear and splashed onto the tip of her smallest son's nose.

'Tish, tish, tishapopple,' said the little tiger. 'That tickled.'

'You must take care that you don't catch a cold,' said the tigress. 'This rain is very dampening ...'

'You can say *that* again ...' said a solemn Australian voice from behind the tiger cub.

'This rain is very dampening ...' said the little cub obediently.

'Oh, very funny I'm sure,' said the voice gloomily. 'It's all very well for you to make fun of me, but it's terrible weather like this that has made me what I am today ...'

He was a very strange creature. He was almost as big as the little tiger cub and covered with scales. He had the most amazing frill round his neck.

'It was like this ...' the creature went on. 'In the good old days my ancestors were the greatest of all the dinosaurs. Chlamydosaurus they called them, and a clammy life it turned out to be. At first they were tall and strong with huge teeth, great spines on their backs and magnificent claws. They had a spike on the end of their tails too and their scales were as golden as the sun on Bondi Beach. Splendid they were, with a roar that could be heard for miles. They used to bask in the sun, lashing their tails to and fro and roaring in a terrifying way from time to time. And then it happened ...'

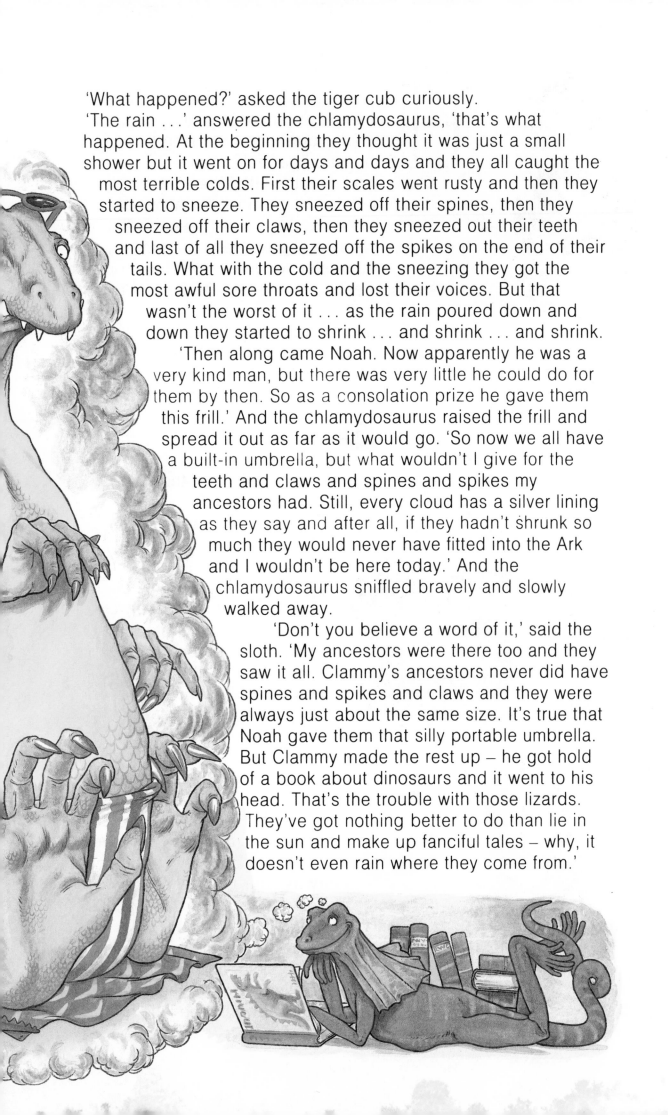

'What happened?' asked the tiger cub curiously.

'The rain . . .' answered the chlamydosaurus, 'that's what happened. At the beginning they thought it was just a small shower but it went on for days and days and they all caught the most terrible colds. First their scales went rusty and then they started to sneeze. They sneezed off their spines, then they sneezed off their claws, then they sneezed out their teeth and last of all they sneezed off the spikes on the end of their tails. What with the cold and the sneezing they got the most awful sore throats and lost their voices. But that wasn't the worst of it . . . as the rain poured down and down they started to shrink . . . and shrink . . . and shrink.

'Then along came Noah. Now apparently he was a very kind man, but there was very little he could do for them by then. So as a consolation prize he gave them this frill.' And the chlamydosaurus raised the frill and spread it out as far as it would go. 'So now we all have a built-in umbrella, but what wouldn't I give for the teeth and claws and spines and spikes my ancestors had. Still, every cloud has a silver lining as they say and after all, if they hadn't shrunk so much they would never have fitted into the Ark and I wouldn't be here today.' And the chlamydosaurus sniffled bravely and slowly walked away.

'Don't you believe a word of it,' said the sloth. 'My ancestors were there too and they saw it all. Clammy's ancestors never did have spines and spikes and claws and they were always just about the same size. It's true that Noah gave them that silly portable umbrella. But Clammy made the rest up – he got hold of a book about dinosaurs and it went to his head. That's the trouble with those lizards. They've got nothing better to do than lie in the sun and make up fanciful tales – why, it doesn't even rain where they come from.'

appy birthday dear,' said the tigress one morning, ' and here is your present.' She pushed a brand new drinking bowl across to the little tiger cub.

'Ooh mum,' said the little tiger, 'it's lovely. I've always wanted a drinking bowl of my own.'

The lioness poked her head round the door of the cage, 'Happy birthday dear,' she purred, 'here's a little present for you ...' And she pushed a brand new eating dish along the floor of the cage towards the cub.

'Ooh,' said the tiger cub, 'an eating bowl of my own too! I do like birthdays!'

All that morning wherever the little tiger cub went he was wished 'many happy returns' and 'a happy birthday' by all the animals. By lunchtime he was quite dizzy and had to lie down in the shade. He was looking up into the leaves when the sloth's mournful voice floated down to him.

'You're looking very pleased with yourself,' said the sloth.

'It's my birthday,' said the tiger cub happily.

'Many happy returns I'm sure,' said the sloth sadly, 'I never have birthdays.'

'Why not?' asked the tiger cub, amazed that someone didn't know what birthdays were like.

'I am an orphan,' said the sloth, 'and orphans don't know when their birthdays are. I don't suppose I'll ever know which day is my birthday, I don't suppose I'll ever know which day I was born and no one can tell me ...' A tear splashed down through the leaves.

'I know!' said the little tiger cub suddenly. 'Why don't you decide that today is your birthday – after all it really might be, and if you choose today as your birthday, I'll always be able to remember it because it's the same as mine.'

'Do you really think so?' said the sloth, and he slowly, slowly climbed down the tree and lay down by the little tiger cub.

'Yes I do,' said the little tiger cub firmly. 'Come along, I'll go and tell my mum.'

Together the two animals went to the tigress and told her all about it. The tigress thought that this was an especially good idea and the sloth joined in the tiger cub's birthday party. All the animals brought presents for both of them and at the end of the day the sloth was actually smiling – really smiling for the first time in his entire life.

That night the tigress and the tiger cub took the sloth back to his tree and wished him goodnight.

'That was a lovely day,' said the sloth. 'I've never had such a lovely day. I really like birthdays, in fact I love them, but do you know something?'

'What's that dear?' said the tigress.

'I've been thinking, and perhaps I was wrong about today being my birthday. Perhaps it is tomorrow, or perhaps it's the day after – I can't be sure can I?'

'I suppose not,' said the tiger cub, yawning widely, doing his best to stay awake.

'Tell you what, said the sloth. 'I'd better have a birthday tomorrow as well, and the day after, just so's I make sure that I don't miss it . . .'

One night the strains of dance music drifted across the zoo as the animals sat in their usual circle. They swayed together, to and fro as the music swirled round them.

'Isn't this romantic?' murmured the zebra to his mate. 'It reminds me of the time when I got my stripes ...'

'Do you remember when we last heard this?' whispered the lion to the lioness.

'Of course I do dear,' she replied softly. 'It was when we were working in the circus.'

And then the music died away, and through the twilight came a crisp voice.

'A-one-two-three-four, a-one-two-three-four, one-two-three-and ...

Into the circle of animals marched an extremely lively dance band, composed entirely of penguins. The emperor penguin led them, conducting as he led. Behind him came eight king penguins, four playing clarinets and four playing trombones. Behind them came eight Adelie penguins, each playing a trumpet. Behind them came eight rockhopper penguins, four playing violins, two playing double basses and two playing guitars – and behind *them*, right at the back, a little blue penguin stumbled on, carrying a complete drum kit and occasionally managing a thump on the big bass drum as he wobbled along.

They arranged themselves in the centre of the circle and the emperor penguin turned to the audience.

'Ladies and gentlemen ...' he announced, 'to celebrate the one hundred and twenty-five thousandth anniversary of the day the Ark landed on Mount Ararat, we proudly present A One Hundred And Twenty-Five Thousandth Anniversary Concert, featuring the same star cast as we had last year to celebrate the one-hundred and twenty-four thousand nine-hundred and ninety-ninth anniversary.

From the back of the orchestra came a great OOMPAH OOMPAH OOOOOMP! and a tiny Galapagos penguin staggered in, almost completely hidden by the most enormous euphonium.

'S.s.s.o.ory I'm l.l.ate,' he said squeakily, 'b.b.ut my instrum.m.m.ent fell on m.m.me and I had to wait for the e.e.e.elephant to c.c.come and p.p.p.ull it off.'

The emperor penguin went on as if nothing had happened.

'Our first act tonight, and by popular request, is a concatenation of carolling chorines, a chirruping celebration of cheeriness – in other words – the CHICKENS' CHORUS!'

The band struck up a rousing tune and a chorus line of chickens danced on, then to a roll of drums a most gorgeous bird swayed into the centre of the stage, turned shyly to the audience and began to sing:

I was only a bird in a gilded cage
But I certainly knew what to do ... to do

When the rain came down and the sky went dark
I followed old Noah right into the Ark
And chirruped away like a high flying lark
'Cause I certainly knew what to do ... to do.

But even a bird in a gilded cage
Has troubles that she must go through ... go through

The price for the voyage that I had to pay
Was breakfast for everyone every day
And three thousand eggs is a great deal to lay
Yes I'd troubles I had to go through ... go through.

After the applause for the Chicken Chorus had died away and the animals had settled down, the master-of-ceremonies turned to the audience again.

'And now, ladies and gentlemen, for your further delectation, a veritable virtuoso – not only a valiant veteran of vaudeville, but a vertiginous ventriloquist … I give you … THE GREAT VULTURO!!!

Into the circle of animals shambled the most disreputable looking bird the tiger cub had ever seen. Completely bald, with ragged and sparse feathers and little eyes peering out of a wrinkled and battered face, he was dressed in a decrepit black frock coat. He sat down and blinked round at his audience. Then, from behind his back he brought out a bright green parrot which he seated on his right knee.

'Who's a pretty boy then?' said the parrot suddenly, turning his head jerkily from side to side. 'Pieces of eight, pieces of eight.'

The vulture's beak didn't move while the parrot spoke and the little tiger cub looked on in amazement.

'Gottle of geer, gottle of geer,' yelled the parrot. And again his head jerked from side to side and his beak snapped open and shut, and yet there wasn't a single movement from the vulture.

An ostrich with pink plumes wearing a sparkling collar came on carrying a glass of water.

'The Great Vulturo will now drink the water while performing!' she lisped, turning from side to side and showing the audience that the glass was indeed filled with water.

The Great Vulturo took the glass and started to drink – the little tiger cub could see that the water in the glass was going down, but all the time the vulture was drinking the parrot was shouting, 'Gread and gutter, gread and gutter, who's a pretty boy then? Pieces of eight, pieces of eight ...'

There was a storm of applause as the vulture handed the empty glass back to the ostrich.

Slowly he got up and bowed to the animals, and slowly he shuffled away while the master-of-ceremonies held up his hand to quieten the applause, ready to announce the next act.

'Wasn't that marvellous mum?' whispered the little tiger cub. 'The Great Vulturo didn't move his beak once! I wonder how he did it. And wasn't the dummy realistic? Oh I wish I could be a ventriloquist like him.'

'Don't be silly dear,' said his mother fondly. 'It was the parrot who was the ventriloquist – the vulture was the dummy!'

The next evening the animals gathered together again to hear another story.

The old lion was just about to begin when a little bird began to chirrup in the background.

'Shhh,' growled the lion, 'I'm about to begin my story.'

'But you always tell boring stories,' said the little bird, and flew down and perched on the lion's head.

'Oh very well,' said the lion. 'You tell one then.'

'Once,' began the little bird, strutting about importantly in the rough curls of the lion's mane.

'Once my ancestors were the most magnificent of all the birds.'

The younger animals muttered disbelievingly.

'They were, they were,' said the little bird, 'as you shall hear. You see that toucan over there. Well he's wearing our beak! It all happened like this . . .' and the animals sat back to listen.

'Gambling,' the bird went on, 'has been the ruin of my family. And the first bet my ever-so-many-greats-great-grandfather made was with the toucan. He bet the toucan that he could sing the loudest. He couldn't of course and so the toucan got the splendid beak and he got a little one in exchange.

'You'd think he would have learned his lesson wouldn't you? Well he didn't, because that very afternoon, he was sitting up a tree admiring his tail when along came a peacock. The peacock was a fairly handsome fellow even then, but nothing to what he is today. Before he knew what had come over him my great-great-ever-so-many greats-grandfather had bet that he could run faster than the peacock. They set off but his tail slowed him down and he lost the race and his splendid tail too.

'Well, the only lovely feathers he had left to his name were those on his breast – cherry red they were and as soft as silk. He was admiring himself in a pool that evening when up came a robin. Now you know how fierce robins are, but before my great-great-ever-so

many-greats-grandfather could help himself he had bet the robin that he could beat him in a fight. He couldn't of course and he lost not only the fight but his red feathers as well. And there he was – brown and speckled and drab.

'But it didn't stop him gambling did it?' said the gnu (who knew everything).

'No it didn't,' said the little speckled bird.

'What happened next?' asked the anteater, who was a very nosy animal.

'Well it was then that the rains started and the animals had to go into the Ark. It was while he was there that he bet Noah that he could make the best house. He knew it was a stupid bet as soon as he opened his beak, but he couldn't stop himself. He lost, of course, and had to give up the only thing he had left – his nest. Yes folks, he gambled away his home!'

A silence fell as the little brown bird finished his story. All the animals who had heard it before nodded wisely, and the younger ones, who hadn't, gasped in horror.

'Lost his home! How awful!'

'Now let that be a lesson to you my dear,' said the tigress to her cub. 'No good ever comes of gambling.'

'Who *is* that little bird mum?' asked the cub.

'That's the cuckoo dear,' she answered, 'and it's just about the right name for him too.'

There was a strange noise coming from the beavers' lodge, a chipping and a hammering, a crashing and a splashing. All the animals gathered round to gaze in amazement at the gigantic dam that the beavers were building.

'What's it for mum?' asked the little tiger.

'I don't know dear,' answered the tigress, 'but it looks very important.'

The tiger cub moved over to the chief beaver who was tugging and pulling at a large log, and trying to put it on top of the dam.

'What are you doing?' asked the tiger cub.

'What does it look like?' answered the beaver, 'We're building a dam, so that when the rain comes we won't be flooded. And Spats says that the rain is coming again.'

'Oh ... Spats,' said the little tiger cub doubtfully. 'What does he know? It's probably a trick.'

Spats McLean the alligator was standing by the dam, looking as if he was admiring the view. Behind him was a large placard on which said:

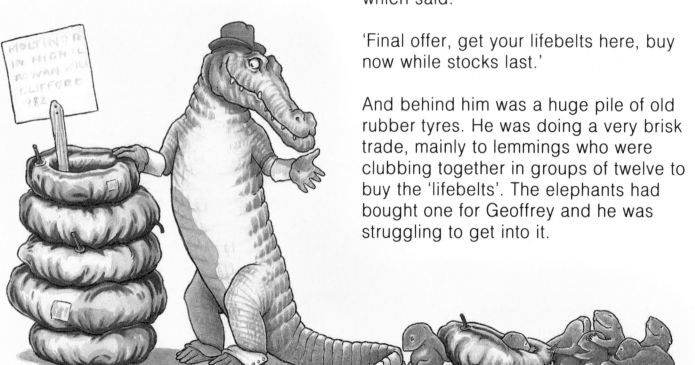

'Final offer, get your lifebelts here, buy now while stocks last.'

And behind him was a huge pile of old rubber tyres. He was doing a very brisk trade, mainly to lemmings who were clubbing together in groups of twelve to buy the 'lifebelts'. The elephants had bought one for Geoffrey and he was struggling to get into it.

'And when is this rain supposed to come Spats?' asked the tiger cub sarcastically, looking up at the cloudless sky.

'This evening son,' said Spats.

And that night, the tiger cub was woken by the sound of falling water. In the morning, the zoo was partly flooded, mainly because the dam that the beavers had built was holding the water back.

That day, Spats did very good trade, selling rubber tyres like hot cakes. Again that night the sound of heavy falling water kept the cub awake. In the morning Spats sold the last of his tyres and disappeared back into the alligator pond. It was just as well, because the tiger cub had been snooping around and discovered, lying behind the elephant house, a huge tangle of hosepipes surrounded by alligator footprints.

When the beavers were told they were furious.

They set to work at once, chopping through the logs in the dam until at last a fine jet of water began to spray through. The animals stood back gleefully as the jet became a thundering torrent and a swirling mass of water churned across the grass to the alligator pond, sweeping all before it. Spats could just be seen, tumbling over and over in the waves, as the animals shouted at him;

'What you need is a lifebelt Spats.
Buy now while stocks last!'

One summer's evening when the zoo was closed for the day, the tiger cub was going to see his friends the elephants when he saw, stretched between the trees which stood by the lion's den, a huge banner, on which was written in curly letters:

TONITE – FOR ONE NITE ONLY –
THE GREAT CHAM!
MASTER OF ILLUSION, MASTER OF DISGUISE!!!

He ran back to ask his mum who the Great Cham was.

'Wait and see, wait and see . . .' his mother replied.

A little later the animals gathered as usual. There was a feeling of excitement in the air, and even the sloth looked lively and interested and wasn't keeping himself to himself for once.

All at once there was a fanfare of trumpeting from the elephants, and the ostrich strode into the centre of the grass just as if it were a stage.

'Ladeees and Gentlemen,' he announced. 'By popular request, and for one night only, we proudly present – THE GREAT CHAM!!'

A line of tigers danced on, and stood at the back of the 'stage', their stripes glowing in the evening light. Then the camel arrived, carrying the baboon on his back. The baboon in turn was carrying a green box.

'Surely the Great Cham can't be in there,' said the tiger cub. 'How can he be great if he can fit into that little box?'

'Hush dear and watch,' said his mother.

With a flourish the baboon placed the box on the grass and with an even larger flourish he opened the lid of the box.

From the box stepped one of the most curious creatures the tiger cub had ever seen. He looked like a little wizened dragon. His skin was a brilliant green and he moved as slowly and carefully as an old woman crossing a road. His eyes were most peculiar. Each one looked where it wanted to, so the Great Cham could see where he was going and watch where he had come from, at the same time.

Carefully, as if his legs were made of glass, the Great Cham came to the centre of the stage and stood before the line of tigers. Then, an amazing thing happened. It happened so slowly that it was difficult to see any change at first. THE GREAT CHAM DISAPPEARED!

'Coo!' gasped the little tiger cub.

The line of tigers danced off and there, standing in exactly the same place as before was the Great Cham. But he was no longer a brilliant green, he was striped just like a tiger.

Now the anteater arrived, carrying a large yellow flag with a red star in the middle, he stood behind the Great Cham and held the flag up as best he could – and again, the Great Cham disappeared!

The anteater left, trailing his flag – and there stood the Great Cham, in exactly the same place as before, but this time he was bright yellow, with a red star across his middle.

'And now, ladees and gentlemen, the Great Cham challenges the audience to find a background against which he cannot disappear.'

All the animals rushed forward, each carrying something brightly coloured which they held up behind the Great Cham. The lion brought out a football jersey that one of the zoo visitors had left behind. It was striped in blue and white, but this presented no difficulty to the Great Cham. Neither did the pink sunhat that one of the flamingoes had found floating on their pond.

And then, from the back of the audience came the hyena. A hiss ran through the animals, for in his mouth the hyena was carrying the head keeper's gardening shirt. The hyena spread it out on the ground and went back to his place, laughing as if he would burst.

'Can the Great Cham beat this?' asked the ostrich.

But there was no answer. The Great Cham had fallen in a faint.

'What's the matter with him?' asked the tiger cub.

'Well dear,' his mother replied, 'even the Great Cham cannot disappear against that. You see, the head keeper is a Scotsman, and his shirt is Royal Stewart Tartan!

There were hundreds of lemmings milling around the grass outside the lion's den one night. They tumbled over each other and bumped into each other and sat in heaps together and snoozed in corners together and crowded round the drinking pool together. The little tiger cub had never seen such busy or friendly animals.

'Isn't it peculiar Mum,' he told his mother, 'they really hate being alone – there isn't a single lemming by himself anywhere.' At that moment the largest lemming cleared his throat. Immediately all the other lemmings cleared their throats and sat up alertly.

'Good evening friends,' began the biggest lemming, and all the other lemmings squeaked 'Good evening, good evening,' just like a furry echo.

'Let me tell you why we lemmings stick together,' the largest lemming went on. 'We do it for our own safety you see. If we hadn't stuck together on that dreadful day when the rain came down, we wouldn't be here now. It was like this . . .' and all the other lemmings murmured "like this, like this . . ." like the wind rustling through a forest.

'When the rain started, the lemmings were scattered all over the icy plains of the north. They didn't pay much attention at first, but when the waters started to rise they certainly noticed then. Well, after a while along came Noah and the message went out that they were to gather ready to board the Ark; but how were they going to get the message to the others? They weren't built for speed you see, it was their legs you know – too short for speed.' And all the lemmings chimed in, "too short, too short".

'First they asked the Arctic fox if he would run their message, and he agreed. He was off like a flash. But when he came back he said that he hadn't found any lemmings to tell, even though he looked much fatter than when he set off. Then they asked the Siberian wolf, and he agreed. But

when he came back he too looked extremely fat and said that he'd found no one to tell. Then they asked the snowy owl and he agreed. But when he returned he was almost too fat to fly, and said that he had hunted high and low but he hadn't found any lemmings to tell, and would they like to spread out and search with him.

'They were all ready to agree when Noah hurried them onto the Ark.

'He asked where the rest of them were, and when they said they didn't know, he said that it was time to set off and they'd pick up any stragglers on the way.

'Well, the waters rose and rose and pretty soon all that was left of the land where they lived, was the top of two Siberian mountains. As the Ark sailed past all the animals saw that the mountains were crowded with lemmings, all squeaking for help like mad and begging to be saved. Noah anchored the Ark as near as he could and shouted to them to swim for it.

'The Arctic foxes and the Siberian wolves and the snowy owls all joined in, but for some peculiar reason, the lemmings left on the land refused to swim out to the Ark. No one was ever able to understand why they wouldn't come on board, even when the Siberian wolf very kindly stood at the top of the gangplank and offered to help them up, and the snowy owl, even though he must have been tired from all that flying, offered to carry some of them aboard in his claws.

'And there it is. Ever since that day we have stuck together, just in case any messages should come through. And sometimes they do – the odd owl sometimes comes to us and tells us to meet at the edge of the sea, and off we rush. But when we get there, all we find are crowds of wolves and foxes … most peculiar.'

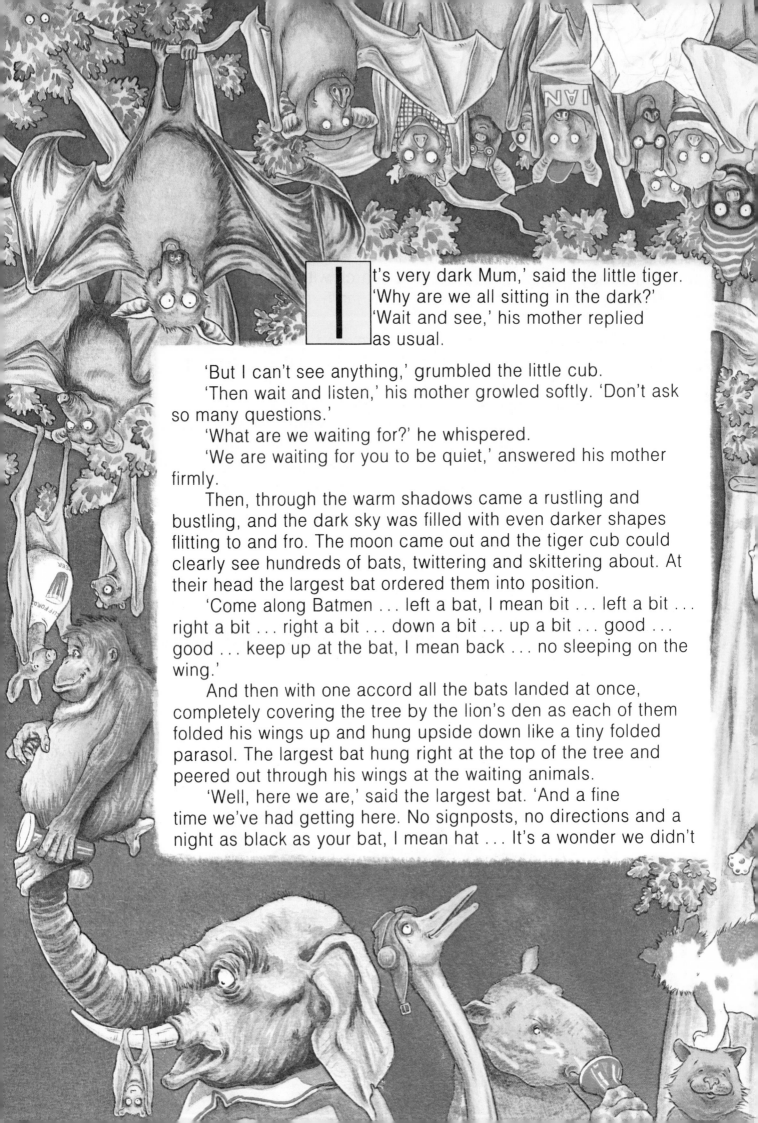

It's very dark Mum,' said the little tiger. 'Why are we all sitting in the dark?' 'Wait and see,' his mother replied as usual.

'But I can't see anything,' grumbled the little cub.

'Then wait and listen,' his mother growled softly. 'Don't ask so many questions.'

'What are we waiting for?' he whispered.

'We are waiting for you to be quiet,' answered his mother firmly.

Then, through the warm shadows came a rustling and bustling, and the dark sky was filled with even darker shapes flitting to and fro. The moon came out and the tiger cub could clearly see hundreds of bats, twittering and skittering about. At their head the largest bat ordered them into position.

'Come along Batmen ... left a bat, I mean bit ... left a bit ... right a bit ... right a bit ... down a bit ... up a bit ... good ... good ... keep up at the bat, I mean back ... no sleeping on the wing.'

And then with one accord all the bats landed at once, completely covering the tree by the lion's den as each of them folded his wings up and hung upside down like a tiny folded parasol. The largest bat hung right at the top of the tree and peered out through his wings at the waiting animals.

'Well, here we are,' said the largest bat. 'And a fine time we've had getting here. No signposts, no directions and a night as black as your bat, I mean hat ... It's a wonder we didn't

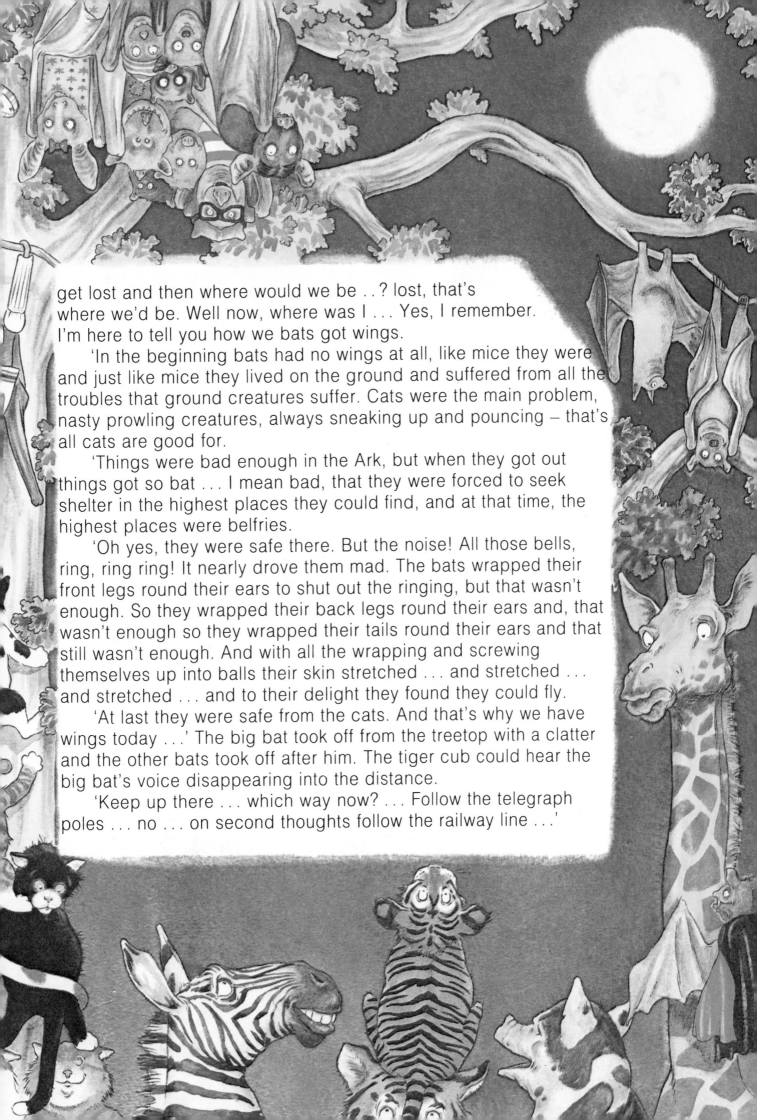

get lost and then where would we be ..? lost, that's where we'd be. Well now, where was I ... Yes, I remember. I'm here to tell you how we bats got wings.

'In the beginning bats had no wings at all, like mice they were and just like mice they lived on the ground and suffered from all the troubles that ground creatures suffer. Cats were the main problem, nasty prowling creatures, always sneaking up and pouncing – that's all cats are good for.

'Things were bad enough in the Ark, but when they got out things got so bat ... I mean bad, that they were forced to seek shelter in the highest places they could find, and at that time, the highest places were belfries.

'Oh yes, they were safe there. But the noise! All those bells, ring, ring ring! It nearly drove them mad. The bats wrapped their front legs round their ears to shut out the ringing, but that wasn't enough. So they wrapped their back legs round their ears and, that wasn't enough so they wrapped their tails round their ears and that still wasn't enough. And with all the wrapping and screwing themselves up into balls their skin stretched ... and stretched ... and stretched ... and to their delight they found they could fly.

'At last they were safe from the cats. And that's why we have wings today ...' The big bat took off from the treetop with a clatter and the other bats took off after him. The tiger cub could hear the big bat's voice disappearing into the distance.

'Keep up there ... which way now? ... Follow the telegraph poles ... no ... on second thoughts follow the railway line ...'

Something has got to be done,' said the tiger cub who still remembered that Spats had tried to cheat him out of the prize for the obstacle race, months before.

'Spats doesn't care about anybody. He does just what he likes, and every time someone else gets cheated.'

'That's right,' squeaked the lemmings. 'What are we going to do with all those rubber tyres he sold us?'

'And what about my coat?' said the tortoise.

'And mine!' said the armadillo.

'And what about the time we were cheated in the obstacle race?' said the gnu twins.

'And us!' said the Galapagos turtle triplets.

'And us, and us, and us!' chimed in the smallest hippo and Geoffrey the elephant.

'Are we all decided then?' said the tiger cub.

'Yes!' shouted all the animals. 'Let's have a council of war.'

The next day, a large tent appeared inside the hippo enclosure. Above it hung a banner which said:

MADAME MARVELA, FORTUNE TELLER EXTRAORDINARY, FREE CONSULTATIONS.

Soon a long queue of animals was waiting outside the entrance, and among them Spats McLean, the alligator. The queue inched forward until by one o'clock it was Spats's turn. He went in and looked around him. It was very gloomy in there, with hardly enough light coming through the canvas to see Madame Marvela, who sat, wrapped up in a striped shawl which almost covered her face.

'Sit down young man,' Madame Marvela commanded in a growly little voice, and show me your feet.'

Spats held out his front foot.

'This is dreadful,' gasped Madame Marvela. 'You have unlucky feet young man. I can see no future ahead of you. I see water and great peril. Beware of the colours green, brown, yellow and grey. Beware of the mornings, afternoons and nights but most of all beware of the evenings – beware of what you eat and drink, beware of the ground and the trees and beware of the sky, beware of all animals and birds and fishes, beware of the Winter, Spring, Summer and Autumn, beware of standing and of falling, there is terrible danger ahead. I can see no more. I have never seen such an unlucky foot.'

Spats had become very pale.

'Is there no hope?' he croaked.

'Very little young man, but I will look in the crystal ball and see if there is anything you can do to save yourself.'

Madame Marvela leant forward and made several mysterious passes in the air over the crystal ball. She peered into it for a long time and then spoke again in her growly little voice.

'There is one thing you can do,' she said. 'I see from my crystal ball that you have not always been as honest as an alligator should be. Perhaps if you made your peace with the animals you have cheated you may have a chance. Yes, I see it more clearly now. You must reform and then you may have a chance.'

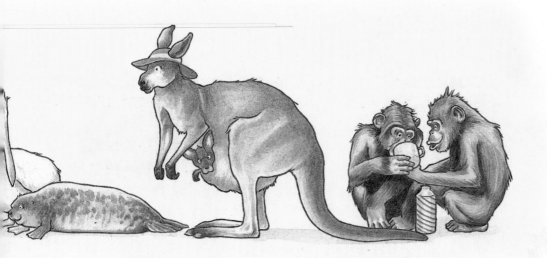

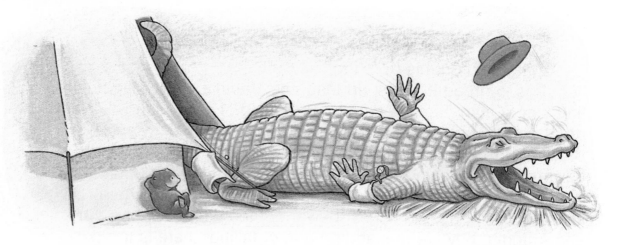

Spats stumbled out of the tent. The sunshine seemed very bright and all round him he could see the colours that Madame Marvela had told him were dangerous. 'It's daytime,' he thought to himself, 'I must beware of that, and of the afternoon, and of the sky.'

He was so busy glancing nervously about him that he did not notice the guy-ropes of the tent and he tripped over them. 'She told me to beware of falling,' he muttered to himself and stumbled on.

He was watching the ground so carefully that he walked into the tree by the lion's den. 'And she told me to beware of trees!' he thought. 'She was right!' He hurried on, looking left and right and up into the sky. Again he missed his footing and fell into the polar bear's pool. 'She told me to beware of water!' he thought as he spluttered his way to the side, 'she was right! I am doomed! I must make my peace with everyone I have cheated and perhaps I can escape my fate.'

For the rest of the afternoon, Spats sought out the animals he had tricked. He gave Geoffrey a huge bag of buns; he took all the rubber tyres back from the lemmings and spent an hour making them into a raft so that the lemmings could practise floating about on the hippo pond. He tidied up the beavers' dam and he went to the tortoise and the armadillo and apologized most humbly for his ancestor's trick, and told them that if there was anything he could do to help them, all they had to do was ask.

He threw a party for the smallest porcupine, the youngest hippo and the gnu twins. He wrote out a public confession which explained that the raccoon's ancestor was innocent. He called his henchmen together and read them moral stories and made them all promise that they would never fall into a life of crime and that they would go about doing good by helping other animals. When

evening came he was so exhausted that he crawled behind the panda's cage.

'Madame Marvela didn't say anything about being beware of this,' he thought as he drifted into sleep. 'Perhaps I'm safe at last!'

That night, as the little tiger cub curled up beside his mother, she said to him.

'Isn't it extraordinary how Spats has reformed. He's a different alligator all of a sudden!'

'Yes,' said the tiger cub sleepily, 'very odd.'

'And there's another strange thing too,' said his mother. 'You wouldn't know anything about that Madame Marvela would you? When I saw her she told me that I had a wonderful son who had a great future ahead of him, but that he needed four meals a day instead of two, and he should be allowed to stay up later at night.'

'She must really be able to see into the future then,' said the little tiger cub, 'because that is eggzackly what you should do.'

M um,' said the little tiger cub, 'I know that emus are birds because it says so outside their pen, but why can't they fly?'

'I don't know dear. Why don't you go and ask them?'

The tiger cub romped across to the emu's pen, stopping only to wish the sloth happy birthday as he always did each morning, in case today might be the day that really was the sloth's birthday.

The emu chicks were bunched together in one corner and their mother bustled about, booming at them in a loud voice.

'Sidney, will you catch up at the back there. And Bruce, stop pecking at Sheila, she's doing her best. And Beverley, stop daydreaming. Now all together, Flap! Flap! Flap!'

She broke off when she saw the little tiger cub. 'Oh these children,' she said to him, 'they'll be the death of me.'

'What are you teaching them?' asked the little tiger cub.

'I'm teaching them to fly, dear. Would you like to join in?'

'But I thought that emus couldn't fly,' said the tiger cub.

'Well we've been a bit unlucky so far,' said the mother emu, 'but we keep on trying. It's just that the chicks are so lazy. They simply will not flap their wings hard enough.'

'Can you fly?' asked the tiger cub.

'Not exactly,' said the mother emu, 'but that's because I have a problem with my weight. But the chicks hardly weigh anything so they should find it quite easy.'

'I don't think I'd be any good at flying, but if you like, I'll join in to encourage them,' said the little tiger cub kindly.

All morning the emu chicks practised running about flapping their wings. The tiger cub ran about with them, jumping as high as he could – and most of the time he jumped higher than the chicks did.

'Hey,' said Sidney, 'you're better at this than we are. When our mum has her afternoon rest, will you teach us to jump like that?'

That afternoon, the little tiger cub led the chicks over to a pile of rocks that lay in the corner of the emu pen.

'Climb up on these,' he told the chicks, 'and when you're at the top, jump as high as you can and flap your wings as hard as you can. Perhaps that will do the trick.'

First Sidney climbed up to the top of the rocks. 'It's very high up here,' he called down to the tiger cub, 'what do I do now?'

'Flap your wings really hard and jump!' shouted the tiger cub.

Sidney did as he was told, but before he jumped he shut his eyes tightly. He sailed through the air and landed in a heap at the bottom and lay very still. The tiger cub rushed over to him.

'Am I dead?' asked Sidney in a tiny voice.

'Of course not,' said the little tiger cub.

'Then why is it all dark?' asked Sidney.

'Because you've got your eyes shut,' answered the tiger cub.

Sidney opened his eyes and gave a little squeak. 'I'm on the ground – did I fly here?'

'Not eggzackly,' said the little tiger cub. 'Try again.'

'No!' said Sidney firmly, 'I just found something out about being an emu. And it's something that explains everything. We're afraid of heights – so afraid that we'd have to fly with our eyes shut. No wonder we can't fly. If we could, we'd fly off and never know where we were and we'd never, ever come home. Mum would hate that. I'll go and tell her all about it.'

The chicks rushed off to find their mother. The tiger cub listened to them chattering to her. He laughed to himself and turned to go back to his own mum. As he did so he could hear the mother emu saying to her chicks.

'Well, just because you can't fly, that's no reason to stop your swimming lessons, or the tree-climbing lessons. . . . .'

ZOO

But this reasoi
buit up—a gree
leaves a scent b
hereforei resorts
pursued, of dou
for somedtaiano
scent behind

Early one morning, long before the zoo opened, a new notice appeared beside the zoo gates. The baboons noticed it first and told the chipmunks all about it, and then of course the news spread like wildfire.

That evening after all the visitors had gone, the tiger cub and his mother strolled over to see it for themselves.

EXHIBITION OF ENDANGERED SPECIES
COMMENCING IN TWO WEEKS

it said, and that was all.

'What's an endangered species Mum?' asked the tiger cub.

'I think it's a sort of bear,' answered his mother, sitting down and scratching her right ear thoroughly. 'But we'd better go and ask Albert.'

Albert was a parrot, and he was supposed to be a hundred years old. He lived in a huge cage by the monkey house and was thought to be very wise by all the other animals.

'Albert,' called the tigress, 'Albert – what's an endangered species?'

'I don't know,' said Albert grumpily. 'Sometimes I think that I'm an endangered species – I'm endangered by everyone asking me silly questions. Now go away and ask someone else.

The tiger cub and his mum walked on, none the wiser. They came to the gorilla's cage. Guy stood there, chewing at a banana.

'Guy,' called the tigress, 'what's an endangered species?'

'I don't know,' said Guy. 'I sometimes feel endangered because I don't get enough bananas. You'd better ask someone else.'

The tigers walked on and came to the porcupine's cage where they asked him if he knew what an endangered species was.

'I don't really know,' he answered. 'I sometimes think I'm a danger to myself, but I wouldn't say I was endangered. You'd better ask someone else.'

The tigers walked on. They came to the pandas' cage where unknown to them, Spats was hiding. The bamboo that grew inside the cage was so high that it was very hard to tell whether the pandas were there or not.

'Do you know what an endangered species is?' called the tigress, peering through the fronds of bamboo.

Behind the back of the cage Spats heard the question. The things that Madame Marvela had told him the day before all came back to him. He remembered that she had said that he was in danger from colours, from the sky, water, standing, falling, daytime, night time, eating, drinking and lots of other things.

'I am,' he called out, 'I'm the most endangered species of all. I'm endangered by everything. I am *definitely* endangered.'

The tigress, thinking that the panda had answered her, turned to her cub and said,

'There you are, the panda's an endangered species. I expect it's because they're so rare. Now come along, it's nearly bedtime.' And she marched him back to their cage, paying no attention to him when he said,

'But Mum, Madame Marvela said ...'

Later that night Spats ventured out from behind the pandas' cage, which was very near to the entrance to the zoo. He saw the notice and it seemed quite right to him that he should be the reason for a special exhibition. He waited for weeks and weeks, but no one seemed to come specially to look at him. They all went to look at the pandas instead.

49

The whole zoo was perfectly quiet when the little tiger woke up the next morning. It was as if everything had been wrapped in silence. The tiger cub stretched and yawned and then blinked – and blinked again. The whole world was different!

'Mum,' he squeaked, 'Mum, come quick! The zoo's gone!'

But his mother only stretched and purred softly and then went back to sleep again.

The little tiger crept out of his cage. The ground was covered with soft, cold, white snow. He rolled over in it, tried to eat it and tried to jump on it, but every time he thought he had caught it, it either slid away from him or melted on his warm pink tongue. He looked behind him and saw his footprints. So he practised walking on the tips of his toes so that he only left tiny marks in the snow – then he tried crossing his front legs over as he walked so that his paw-marks were the wrong way round.

He was thinking so hard about what he was doing that he didn't notice the gnu standing mournfully under the eaves of the elephant house.

'Hello there little'un,' said the gnu gloomily. 'Are you coming to the snow statue contest?'

'Yes please,' said the little tiger cub. And they set off through the snow to the place where the zebras lived.

'What is a snow statue contest?' asked the tiger cub.

'It's a contest to find the best statue made of snow,' answered the gnu. 'Here we are.'

The zebra enclosure was covered with a thick layer of snow and three immense snow statues.

'The contest will now be judged,' announced the emperor penguin, 'and I shall be the judge.'

He waddled over to the first contestant – the ring-tailed lemur, who was standing by his statue.

'Five out of ten,' said the penguin sternly, and moved on to the next entry.

'And what is this then?' he asked the smirking warthog who was standing by it.

'It's a work of modern art,' answered the warthog. 'It shows the triumph of the hippopotamus over the mud he wallows in.'

'Two out of ten,' said the penguin, and moved on to the final entry.

The third statue was magnificent, a white snow elephant that stood proudly trumpeting to the sky, perfect in every detail; beside it stood its creator – Spats McLean the alligator.

'Now this is splendid!' said the emperor, 'such detail, such a feeling for form and shape! And is it all your own work?'

Spats looked modestly at his feet.

'Indeed yes, sir,' he answered. 'I toiled at it all night.'

'I hereby announce the winner,' shouted the emperor penguin. 'It is Spats McLean!'

A ripple of applause came from the animals as they made their way back to the warmth of their dens and cages, leaving the little tiger cub gazing up at the wonderful snow elephant.

Suddenly a monstrous sneeze echoed around the white zoo, and a chunk of snow slid from the back of the statue, leaving a peculiar grey patch. Another sneeze and two grey ears appeared, and then another enormous sneeze caused a cascade of snow which revealed a real elephant shivering miserably in the icy air.

'Well ...' he said, looking down at the cub, 'did Spats win then?'

'Yes he did,' said the tiger cub disgustedly. 'And to think that we all believed that he had made a real statue!'

'As you can see, he didn't,' said the elephant sadly. 'He frightened me into standing here all night while the snow covered me ... I didn't dare to move. You'd think he'd have learned by now, wouldn't you. But I suppose an alligator can't change his spats.'

That evening the animals huddled together trying to keep warm. The sun had set early and in the calm evening light the clouds looked heavy and swollen. The tiger cub looked up at the sky, and as he did so a snowflake landed on his nose. The tiger cub crossed his eyes to see what it was, but almost as soon as it had landed, the snowflake melted.

'What was that Mum?' he asked. 'First it was there and then – it wasn't.'

'That's a snowflake dear,' the tigress told him, 'and when it snows the whole world changes – just like it was this morning. Now sshh, the polar bear is about to begin his story.'

'Isn't this lovely weather?' began the polar bear. 'More what I'm used to. Now I'm going to tell you the tale of my great-great-great-great-great-great-great-ever-so-many-greats grandmother, and how her coat changed from brown to white overnight. In the days before the flood, when all the world was green and peaceful, we polar bears had black or brown coats, just like all other bears. Then that dreadful day came and it began to rain. All the other animals took advantage of Noah's offer and clambered onto the Ark – but not my great-great-ever-so-many-greats grandmother – on no! She was as stubborn as they come.

'"You'll not get me on one of those new-fangled things," she told my great-great-ever-so-many-greats grandfather. "It's not natural. It goes to a point at the bottom and it's very, very heavy. It'll never float – you mark my words." So while my great-great-ever-so-many-greats grandfather lived in comfort on the Ark, she was busy running away from the waters as they rose. First the equator was flooded, so she went north. Then the tropics were flooded so she had to go even further north. And then the water covered all the lands as far as the cold

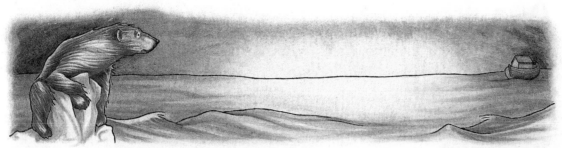

polar seas and my great-great-ever-so-many-greats grandmother had to swim for it. And all the time, Noah was following her in the Ark. The other animals leaned over the sides and jeered at her and took bets on how long she would last in the icy water – all, that is, except my great-great-ever-so-many-greats grandfather. He stayed below and wrapped himself up in all the blankets he could find.

'This went on for days, until the water became so cold it began to freeze. The Ark made heavy going of it, and at last Noah had to give up. By now my great-great-ever-so-many-greats grandmother was sitting on an ice floe and laughing at all of us. She floated away into the distance as the Ark turned round and headed for warmer water.

'You can imagine how my great-great-ever-so-many-greats grandfather felt! Left behind without his mate, and everyone saying that she had left him because he was so difficult to live with. Well, when the waters went down and all the animals left the ark, my great-great-ever-so-many-greats grandfather took off to find her.

It took him several years and what with all the worry his hair went completely white. But at last he did find her, safe and well amongst the icebergs and the snow fields.'

'But you said you would tell us how your great-great-ever-so-many-greats grandmother went white overnight – not your great-great-ever-so-many-greats grandfather,' said the little tiger cub. 'Why did *she* go white?'

'It was the shock of seeing great-great-ever-so-many-greats grandfather after all that time,' said the polar bear seriously. 'She'd got used to living on her own by then you see, and the truth of it was, that she wouldn't have minded going on the Ark at all really. It was just that she saw it as her only chance to get away from great-great-ever-so-many-greats grandfather at last!'

How quiet it is,' whispered the little tiger cub. 'Why isn't anyone saying anything?'

'Hush dear,' his mother told him. 'We're all waiting.'

'What for?' asked the cub.

'Wait and see,' said his mother.

A stork marched into the centre of the circle of animals, 'Atten . . . SHUN!' he announced importantly. 'He's coming . . . any minute now . . .'

'Who's coming?' asked the little tiger cub: but his mother would only say, 'wait and see, wait and see . . .'

A wallaby bounced into the ring of waiting animals. He tripped over his back legs, tumbled down in a heap, picked himself up, found he was looking the wrong way, spun round and fell over again,

'He's coming, he's coming,' he shouted in a muffled voice from amongst his tangled legs. 'It won't be long now . . .'

'But *who*'s coming?' asked the tiger cub. 'Why won't you tell me?'

'Look – ' his mother commanded.

The little tiger cub looked – and gasped in amazement. A line of splendid peacocks came into the centre of the circle, spreading their tails out and bowing their shining heads until they looked like a brilliant sea blue and green. All at once and all together they raised their tails until all the eyes in their tail feathers looked back over their shoulders at . . .

'Who is *that*?' gasped the tiger cub.

'I don't know dear,' whispered his mother. 'None of us do. All we have been told is that the lion must give up his crown because we are to have a new King of the Animals . . .'

In the centre of the gleaming circle of peacocks stood the most fantastic animal the tiger cub had ever seen. Almost as big as the elephant and with a mane longer than the lion, the creature had pink wings and his head was covered with a mass of silvery yellow plumes through which ten strong teeth shone.

'It's beautiful' said a lemming.

'Bit bright,' remarked a bat from its perch high above.

'More than a bit,' hissed the rattlesnake.

'Can it climb trees?' asked the sloth.

'Not with these feet,' replied the wallaby. 'It can hardly walk.'

'Looks very odd to me,' said a penguin.

'And me,' said another.

About the creature's shoulders was a magnificent mane of swaying golden hair and behind him stretched three tails, each tipped with an explosion of green feathers. But it was his four pairs of legs that were the most amazing of all – one pair was especially long and sturdy with the feet planted firmly on the ground.

'Ahem, ahem,' the first peacock began. 'May I present to you the great and mighty Paradiso, your new king and master. He is stronger than the elephant. He can soar higher than the eagle. He can sing more sweetly than the nightingale. No more shall the king of the beasts be confined to the ground as the lion is. This is the shape of things to come – Do you accept your new king?'

The animals fell silent. They were so used to the lion being their king that the idea of any other creature ruling over them seemed strange and disturbing. 'Will he be kind? Will he be fair?' They asked themselves.

'Come, come,' said the peacock, who seemed to be strangely flustered. 'Make up your minds – accept him as your ruler . . .'

Suddenly one of the tails of the strange creature twitched and the tiger cub thought for a moment that there was something very peculiar about this new king.

And the tiger cub was not the only one who saw it.

'Ooooh . . .' said the animals. And the wind their voices made blew the mass of silver yellow plumes on the creature's head, revealing its teeth to be no more than the beaks of ten budgerigars who had been crouching under the tails of five birds of paradise.

'Aaaah . . .' said the animals. And the wind of their voices blew the mane of swaying golden hair, revealing that the three tails were no more than the necks of three flamingoes who were holding large bunches of feathery green leaves in their beaks and who had been hiding under the tails of five more birds of paradise.

'Eeeeh . . .' said the animals. And the ostrich, fully revealed for what he was took to his heels followed closely by the other twenty-three parts of the would-be king of the beasts.

'Well, well, what do you think of that?' said the tigress. But her little cub wasn't listening. He was stamping about with two tortoises and a tabby cat on his back, shouting,

'I'm the king of the animals, I'm the king of the animals. . . .'

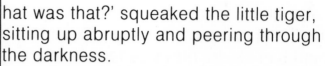

What was that?' squeaked the little tiger, sitting up abruptly and peering through the darkness.

'Nothing dear,' mumbled his mother, 'go back to sleep.'

But the little tiger couldn't go back to sleep. He was sure that he had heard something, and he was sure that he could hear rustlings and bumpings coming from the other side of the lions' den. Carefully, so that he didn't wake up his mother, he slipped out of his cage and started off through the darkness to the lion's den. He had hardly gone three paces when he heard the bump again.

'Who's there?' he whispered.

'No one,' a voice whispered back, 'go back to sleep.' The little tiger cub didn't want to go to sleep. He crept on. He had only gone two paces further when he felt a movement beside him. It was very faint, no more than a breath of air, but he stopped and asked again,

'Who's there.'

And a different voice answered, 'No one, go back to your cage.'

'I was sure I felt something,' he thought to himself, 'but perhaps I was wrong ...'

He crept on again until a little further he stumbled and fell against what felt like the rough bark of a tree. But this 'tree' moved away from him.

'What's that?' he asked nervously.

'Nothing,' came the answer, 'go back to sleep ...'

The tiger cub crept about through the whole night, hearing clumpings and bumpings, rustlings and whisperings, but every time he asked who was there or what it was, back came the answer, 'nothing,' or 'nobody' of 'go back to sleep dear.'

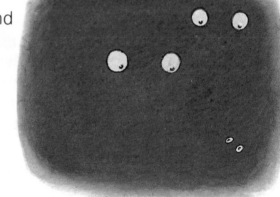

At last the tiger cub gave up and went back to his cage and settled down beside his mother to sleep for what was left of the night.

He had funny dreams all night about ghosts and funny noises and things that go bump in the night.

58

But when he woke up he was amazed! The whole zoo was covered with paper chains, and by the lions' den there was a huge Christmas tree with hundreds of parcels round the base.

'I know who I heard last night,' the tiger cub told his mother.

'Who was that dear?' she asked.

'It was Santa Claus, and what's more I know his other names.'

'And what are they dear,' asked his mother as she smiled down at him.

'Nobody, and Nothing, and Go Back To Sleep Dear,' said the little tiger cub. 'And happy Christmas Mum.'

The tree by the lion's den was almost completely covered with decorations and the bird of paradise was perched on top of it. All the animals had opened their presents and had come out of their cages and pens showing everyone else what Father Christmas had brought them. The only ones that were nowhere to be seen were the turkeys. Every year from the beginning of December they made themselves very scarce, hardly ever coming out of the bird house!

'Look what I got,' said Spats McLean proudly, showing everyone a magnificent pair of bright red spats. 'I'll keep them for special occasions, like birthdays and parties.'

'Who ever asks you to a party?' said Geoffrey's father who still remembered all the money that the buns had cost him on Sports Day, when Spats had assured him that Geoffrey would win the obstacle race.

'Stop bickering you two,' the tigress said. 'Oh look, here comes the penguin band.'

The penguins marched into the centre of the zoo and began to play Christmas carols. All the animals gathered round and had a wonderful time singing their favourite songs.

When they had finished Spats surprised everyone by giving them large crackers. 'Don't ask where they came from,' he said. 'Just pull them and have fun.'

'Come on Geoffrey,' said the tiger cub. 'Pull.'

They pulled and pulled, and suddenly there was a loud bang as the cracker exploded. They were quite surprised when a lemming dropped out.

'Merry Christmas, Geoffrey,' said the tiger cub.

'Merry Christmas everyone,' shouted Geoffrey.

'Merry Christmas, Spats,' said Geoffrey's father.

'I've been thinking, said Spats. 'If you want to make sure that Geoffrey wins the obstacle race next Sports Day . . .'

'Spats!' growled the tigress.

'Merry Christmas,' said Spats.

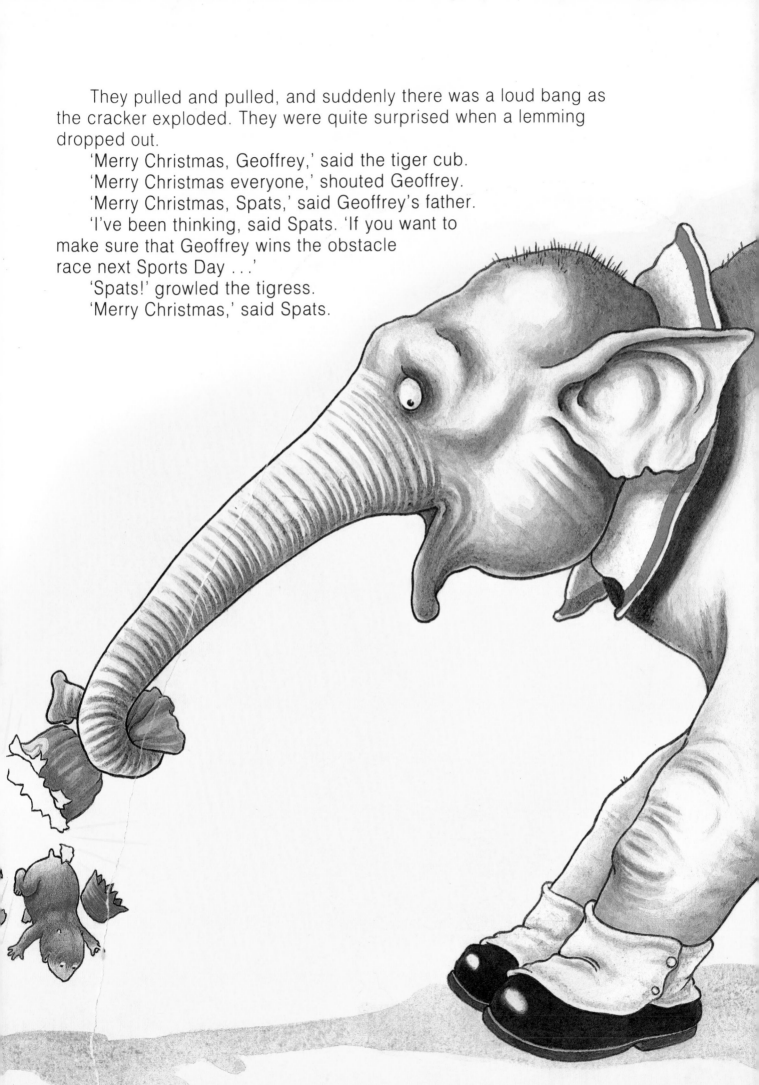

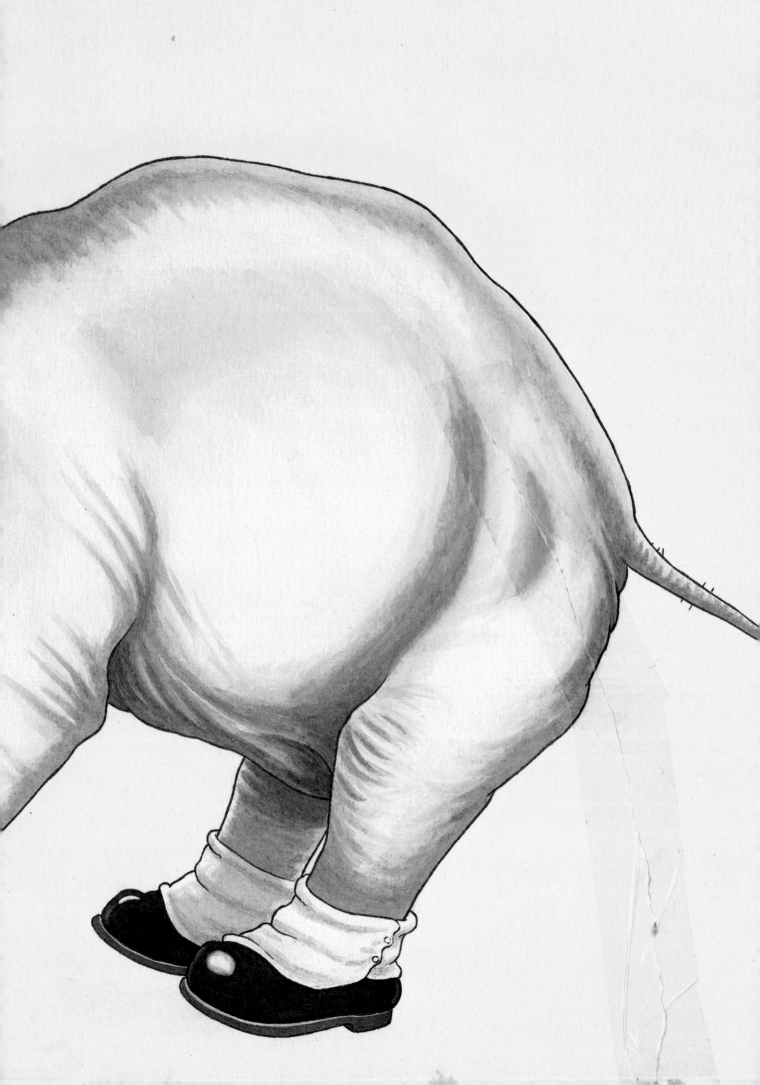